To Sheila, the one who found me. — SB

In memory of my grandma and her visit
to Canada. — QL

Text copyright © 2019 by Saumiya Balasubramaniam
Illustrations copyright © 2019 by Qin Leng
Published in Canada and the USA in 2019 by Groundwood Books

Groundwood Books / House of Anansi Press
groundwoodbooks.com

We gratefully acknowledge for their financial support of our publishing
program the Canada Council for the Arts, the Ontario Arts Council and the
Government of Canada.

Canada Council   Conseil des Arts
for the Arts   du Canada

ONTARIO ARTS COUNCIL
CONSEIL DES ARTS DE L'ONTARIO
an Ontario government agency
un organisme du gouvernement de l'Ontario

With the participation of the Government of Canada
Avec la participation du gouvernement du Canada | Canadä

Library and Archives Canada Cataloguing in Publication
Balasubramaniam, Saumiya, author
When I found Grandma / Saumiya Balasubramaniam ; [illustrated by]
Qin Leng.
Issued in print and electronic formats.
ISBN 978-1-77306-018-7 (hardcover). — ISBN 978-1-77306-019-4 (PDF)
I. Leng, Qin, illustrator II. Title.
PS8603.A47W43 2019   jC813'.6   C2018-903420-3
C2018-903421-1

The illustrations were done in ink and watercolor.
Design by Michael Solomon
Printed and bound in Malaysia

FSC
www.fsc.org
MIX
Paper from
responsible sources
FSC® C012700

When
I Found
Grandma

Saumiya Balasubramaniam

PICTURES BY Qin Leng

Groundwood Books
House of Anansi Press
Toronto   Berkeley

"I wish my grandma came," I said to Mother as we walked home from school one day.

Kim's grandma picked her up every day. My grandma sent postcards in the mail.

"Maya, Grandma lives many thousands of miles away," said Mother.

On our way home from school a few weeks later, Mother said, "I have a surprise for you!"

"Cupcakes?"

"More special," said Mother.

My special surprise wore a crimson sari and carried homemade sweets.

I ran to Grandma. She pinched my cheeks and kissed her fingers. Then she sat cross-legged on the floor and handed out her goodies.

"For you," she said.

I tasted her treats. I liked cupcakes better.

The next day at home
time, Grandma marched
into my classroom, waving.
Her glass bangles jingled
wildly.

Isabella waved back.

"Wait outside, Grandma!" I whispered. "And why
are you still in those fancy clothes?"

"What fancy?" she said, clutching my fingers.

"Don't hold me," I said, and I ran ahead.
She ran after me, yelling, "Mayalakshmi …"

"*Sshhh*," I said. "And call me *Maya*."

"What *ssshhh*? What are you, a pressure cooker?"

That evening, Grandma cooked a meal with rice and cashews.

I pushed the nuts to the side of my plate.

Grandma picked them up with her fingers and brought them to my lips.

"They're good for you, Mayalakshmi," she said.

"STOP, Grandma," I said. "My name is Maya!"

"Don't talk to your elders like that," said Father sharply.

I could not fall asleep that night. Grandma was sitting on her bed peeking at me.

She tiptoed into my room. I squeezed my eyes shut.

Grandma joined her palms and prayed.

"Now you'll sleep well," she said.

"I *am* sleeping," I said, with my eyes still shut.

I woke up to the sound of her prayer bells the next morning. When Grandma disappeared for her super-long shower, I hid the bells under her bed.

But I was excited to be awake. It was spring break. Father had promised a trip to the island.

But why was he dressed in white, looking like Mr. Snowman?

"Happy Holi," cheered Mother, Father and Grandma. When their voices came together, it was very loud — like Grandma's bells.

I remembered celebrating the festival of colors at the temple last year.

"Hurry," said Mother. "Grandma wants to pray at the temple."

A warm teardrop trickled down my cheek.

I ran back into my room. How could they do this to me? I wished Grandma had never come.

After a few minutes, Grandma walked in.
"We could pray on the island," she said.
"On the island?"
"Yes," said Grandma. "Strong prayers come from honest hearts."
"I can't wait to go on the carousel!" I said.

Mother packed cupcakes. Grandma put
on a pair of red pants and blue shoes that
she borrowed from Mother.

At the pier, she bought a baseball cap that matched her pants. She called it her "all-American hat."

When we reached the
island, I let go of Grandma's
hand and raced to the carousel.
Then I turned to show Grandma
my favorite pony. And that's when I saw tall,
small, old, young and all sorts of people, but
none from my family.

The world around me whirled noisily.
The Ferris wheel looked like a monster
with many mouths.

I closed my eyes and tried to pray honestly.
Then I heard a loud voice.
"Mayalakshmi …"
I opened my eyes and looked around.

Mayalakshmi!!!

A red-and-blue cap bobbed in the distance, high over people's heads. Grandma had put her all-American hat over her cane and was holding it up like a balloon.

"Maya," she yelled. "Not Mayalakshmi!"

I walked in the
direction of her hopping
hat. Soon I spotted her
head under the cane.

"Maya!" said Grandma softly.
Grandma could whisper!
She closed her eyes and hugged me.
This time she kissed my cheeks.
I clutched her fingers.

We walked toward the ticket booth where Mother
and Father were waiting.

"I told you I'd find her near the merry-go-round,"
said Grandma.

"Carousel," I said. "And I found you, Grandma."
"You found each other," said Father.
Grandma hoisted her hat, smiling.

That evening, Grandma made rice with cashews again. She said that I wouldn't know the true taste of anything until I tried it three times.

So I tasted some nuts.

They weren't so bad.

At the end of spring break,
Grandma had to go home — many
thousands of miles away.

I lay awake in bed for a long time the night after she left. Then I saw Grandma's bells under her bed.

I stepped into her room. There was a note under the bells.

Keep the bells safe, Maya, it said.

I jingled them gently. They sounded like the sweet tinkle of Grandma's bangles.

The next day at home time, an old lady in a
black dress stepped inside my classroom.
  "Bella," she said, waving.
  "Ssshh, Nonna," said Isabella. "Not so loud."
  "That's okay," I said to Isabella, and I waved
to her grandma.